It's a Dog's Life

Michael Morpurgo

Illustrated by Hannah George

Reading Ladder

Open one eye.

Same old basket, same old kitchen.

Another day.

Ear's itching.

Have a good scratch.

Lovely.

Have a good stretch.

Here comes Lula.

'Morning, Russ,' she says. 'Do you know what day it is today?'

Silly question! Of course I do!

It's the day after yesterday and the day before tomorrow.

Out I go. Smarty's barking his 'good morning' at me from across the valley. Good old Smarty. Best friend I've got, except Lula of course. I bark mine back. I can't hang about. Got to get the cows in.

There they are.

Lula's dad likes me to have them ready for milking by the time he gets there.

Better watch that one with the new calf.
She's a bit skippy. Lie down, nose in the grass.
Give her the hard eye.

There she goes, in amongst the rest.

And here comes Lula's dad,

singing his way down to the dairy.

'Good dog,' he says.

I wag my tail. He likes that.

He gives me another 'good dog'.

I get my milk. Lovely.

Off back up to the house.

Well, I don't want to miss my breakfast, do I?

Lula's already scoffing her bacon and eggs.

I sit down next to her and give her my very

best begging look. It always works.

Two bacon rinds in secret under the table,

and all her toast crusts too. Lovely.

There's good pickings under the baby's
chair this morning.
I hoover it all up. Lovely.

Lula always likes me to go with her to the
end of the lane. She loves a bit of a cuddle,
and a lick or two before the school bus comes.
'Oh, Russ,' she whispers. 'A horse. It's all
I want for my birthday.'

And I'm thinking, 'Excuse me, what's so great about a horse? Isn't a dog good enough?' Then along comes the bus and on she gets. 'See you,' she says.

Lula's dad is whistling for me. 'Where are

you, you old rascal you?'

I'm coming. I'm coming.

Back up the lane, through the hedge,

over the gate.

'Don't just sit there, Russ. I want those sheep in for shearing.'

And all the while he keeps on with his whistling and his whooping.

I mean, does he think I haven't done
this before?

Doesn't he know this is what I'm made for?

Hare down the hill. Leap the stream.
Get right around behind them.

Keep low. Don't rush them. That's good.

They're all going now. The whole flock of them are trotting along nicely.

And I'm slinking along behind, my eye on every one of them, my bark and my bite deep inside their heads.

'Good dog,' I get. Third one today. Not bad.

I watch the shearing from the top of the hay barn. Good place to sleep, this. Tigger's somewhere here. I can smell her. There she is, up on the rafter, waving her tail at me. She's teasing me. I'll show her.

Later, I'll do it later.

Sleep now.

Lovely.

'Russ! Where are you, Russ? I want these sheep out. Now! Move yourself.'

All right, all right. Down I go, and out they go, all in a great muddle bleating at each other, bopping one another.

They don't recognise each other without their clothes on. Not very bright, that's the trouble with sheep.

Look at that! There's hundreds of crows out in my corn field.

Well, I'm not having that, am I? After them! Show them who's boss!

Thirsty work, this.

What's this? Fox!

I can smell him. I follow him down through the bluebell wood to his den. He's down there, deep down. Can't get at him. Pity.

Need a drink.

Shake myself dry in the sun.

Time for another sleep.

Lovely.

Smarty wakes me. I know what he's thinking. How about a Tigger hunt?

We find her soon enough.
We're after her.
We're catching her up.
Closer. Closer. Right on
her tail.

That's not fair. She's found a tree.

Up she goes.

We can't climb trees, so we bark

our heads off.

Ah well, you can't

win them all.

'Russ, where were you, Russ?'

It's Lula's dad, shouting for me again.

'Get those calves out in the field. What's

the point in keeping a dog and barking

myself?'

Nothing's worse than trying to move young calves. They're all tippy-toed and skippy. Pretty things. Pity they get so big and lumpy when they get older.

There, done it. Well done, me!

Back to the end of the lane to meet Lula.

I'm a bit late. She's there already, swinging her bag and singing.

'Happy birthday to me,

    happy birthday to me.

Happy birthday, dear Lula,

    happy birthday to me!'

For tea there's a big cake with candles on it, and they're singing that song again.

Look at them tucking into that cake!

And never a thought for me.

Lula's so busy unwrapping her presents
that she doesn't even notice I'm there,
not even when I put my head on her knee.

Car! A car coming up my lane, and not
one I know. I'm out of the house in a flash.

I'm not just a farm dog, you know, I'm a guard dog too.

'Russ! Stop that barking, will you?'

That's all the thanks I get.

I'm telling you, it's a dog's life.

Looks like a horse to me.

Give him a sniff.

Yes, definitely a horse.

Lula goes mad.

She's hugging the horse just like she hugs me, only for longer. A lot longer.

'He's beautiful,' she's saying. 'Just what I wanted.'

Well, I'm not staying where I'm not wanted.
I haven't had any of that cake, and they're
not watching.
Nip back inside. Jump on a chair.
I'm a champion chomper.

Oops. The plate's fallen off the table.

I'm in trouble now.

They all come running in. I look dead
innocent. Doesn't fool them, though.

'You rascal, you. Out you go!'

I don't care. It was worth it.

I go and sit at the top of the hill
and tell Smarty all about it.
He barks back, 'Good on you!
Who wants to be a good dog,
anyway?'

Then Lula's sitting down beside me.

'I really love my horse,' she says,

'but I love you more, Russ. Promise.'

Give her a good lick. Make her giggle.

I like it when she giggles.

Lick her again.

Lovely.